Bibi Dumon Tak is a Dutch author who has written a number of books for young readers, including two titles published by Eerdmans, *Mikis and the Donkey* and *Soldier Bear*, both of which won the Mildred L. Batchelder Award. She lives in the Netherlands.

Annemarie van Haeringen has created many children's books, including *Mr. Matisse and His Cutouts* (NorthSouth). She is a three-time winner of the Gouden Penseel (Golden Paintbrush) award, the most important Dutch prize for illustration. She lives in the Netherlands. Visit her website at www.annemarievanhaeringen.nl.

Laura Watkinson translated Bibi Dumon Tak's award-winning titles *Mikis and the Donkey* and *Soldier Bear* (both Eerdmans). She lives in the Netherlands.

For Robbie, Jan Paul, Saar, and Loutje

First published in the United States in 2018 by
Eerdmans Books for Young Readers,
an imprint of Wm. B. Eerdmans Publishing Co.
2140 Oak Industrial Dr. NE, Grand Rapids, Michigan 49505
www.eerdmans.com/youngreaders

Text copyright © 2016 Bibi Dumon Tak
Illustrations copyright © 2016 Annemarie van Haeringen
Originally published in the Netherlands in 2016 by Em. Querido's
Kinderboeken Uitgeverij under the title *Siens hemel*.
English language translation © 2018 Laura Watkinson

Manufactured in China

27 26 25 24 23 22 21 20 19 18   1 2 3 4 5 6 7 8 9

ISBN 978-0-8028-5500-8

A catalog record of this book is available from the Library of Congress.

MIX
Paper from
responsible sources
FSC
www.fsc.org   FSC® C104723

Nederlands
letterenfonds
dutch foundation
for literature

Publication was aided by a subsidy from
the Dutch Foundation for Literature and
the Mondriaan Foundation.

Bibi Dumon Tak & Annemarie van Haeringen

Translated by Laura Watkinson

Scout's Heaven

Eerdmans Books for Young Readers

Grand Rapids, Michigan

There were dark clouds in the sky when Scout left.
The sky grumbled.
The rain rumbled.
But all we heard was Scout's last breath, her very last breath
whistling over the edge of her basket.

We let her go, walked to the window, and threw it open.

We felt the rain hitting our faces.

Just for a moment, the clouds slid apart, as if to let Scout slip through,

straight into heaven.

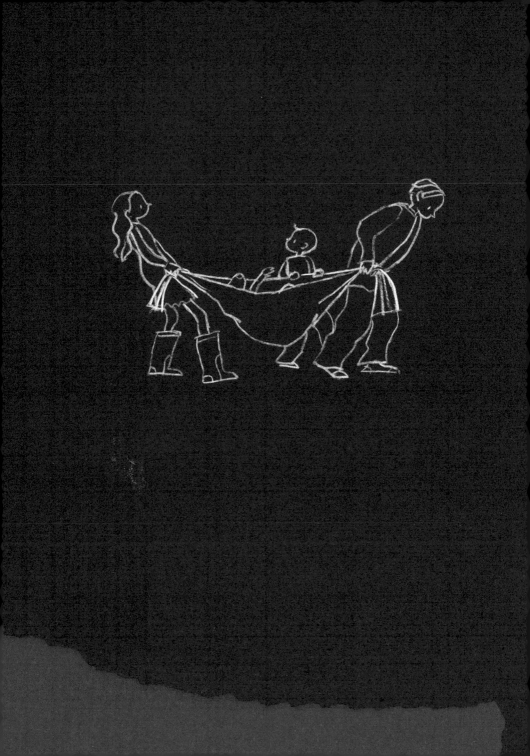

"What now?" Little Brother looked at us with a question on his face.
He pointed up at the heavens and then at the basket.
We nodded, because Little Brother was right:
Scout was there, and Scout was here.
She was in two places at once, and we were in between.
"What now?" we repeated his words. "Now we find a blanket and
we lay Scout on it and we take her outside."

Little Brother paused in the doorway.

"What are you waiting for?" we asked.

"For the rain to stop," he said.

But we didn't wait. We started digging a hole in the ground.
The whole time we were digging, the rain beat on our backs.
We didn't notice it until Little Brother came to stand beside us
and took off his coat to cover Scout.

"Why?" we asked.

"Because," he said.

We scattered leaves and grass on the bottom
of the hole and laid Scout down on them.
"Wait," said Little Brother.
He ran off and came back with a ball.
"In case she wants to play up there."
He pointed at the sky, where the rain
was still falling as if the sun had never existed.

The rain poured down as we covered Scout with earth.
The rain fell on our heads, ran down our faces, our necks,
our arms, legs and feet, and into the earth.
Little Brother wanted to know if it was raining above the clouds too.
"No," we said, "it's dry above the clouds. Why do you ask?"
"Because," said Little Brother, "Scout would get double wet then—
in the ground and in heaven. That's why."

We filed back into the house,
with Little Brother running ahead.
As if he would find Scout there again, behind
the door, napping in the hallway, as always.
Just like every other day of his life.

He took her leash from the hook and held it up.
He asked what we should do with it now.
We shrugged, because we didn't know.
"What about her basket? And her bowl?" he asked.
"Is anyone up there giving Scout her food?"
"We don't know," we answered, and we
wrapped our arms around Little Brother.

We made hot chocolate while
the rain went on falling
and the sky slowly grew dark.
"Can you hear that?" Little Brother asked.
"Hear what?" we replied.
"That growling noise," he said.

"It's thunder," we said, "just thunder
rumbling away in the distance."
Were we sure, Little Brother wanted to know,
were we really sure it wasn't Scout standing outside
and growling at the mail carrier?
And we shook our heads and said
the mail carrier had already come.

We made a big bed
on the rug in the living room,
with Little Brother between us.
He asked if Scout was sleeping
now too. Wasn't she cold
in the wet ground?

Was there a sea in heaven where she
could swim? And enough sticks
for her to gnaw to pieces?
Could she dig a hole up there?
Did it snow where Scout was now?

Could she chase cats?
Pigeons?
Ducks?
Crows?
Cows?
"Why don't you go to sleep?" we said.

"Can she run across the clouds?
Is there someone to pet her?"
Little Brother didn't stop.
"We don't know," we said.
"We don't know what's up there."
So when would we know?
"Tomorrow," we said. "Maybe tomorrow."

Waking up was different.
Not with a wagging tail beating on the bedcovers,
but the sun shining into the room.
We stood up and walked outside, Little Brother leading the way.
"Listen," he said, "I can hear barking."
We pretended to listen.
We did it for Little Brother, to be nice.
Just to play along for a bit.
And when we turned our faces to the sky, we heard it too.
We really did.

We heard barking.

It was coming straight from the clear blue heavens.